## Tomboy in a Dress

"This dress looks great on you, Billie," Jessica exclaimed. "Don't you think so, Elizabeth? Why, it'll make Ji—" She put her hand over her mouth. "It'll make every boy at the party look at you."

Elizabeth's eyes bored through her sister, but Billie didn't notice. She wasn't at all sure she liked the idea of every boy looking at her—unless they were admiring her fastball, that is. She turned around in front of the mirror, and the thought of Jim crept back into her mind. If she could barely recognize herself, what would Jim say when he saw her all dressed up? The thought made her cheeks flush pink from dread and anticipation. . . .

D0962881

Bantam Skylark Books in the SWEET VALLEY TWINS series
Ask your bookseller for the books you have missed

Sweet Valley Twins Super Editions

# SWEET VALLEY TWINS

# *Standing Out*

Written by
Jamie Suzanne

Created by
FRANCINE PASCAL

A BANTAM SKYLARK BOOK®
TORONTO · NEW YORK · LONDON · SYDNEY · AUCKLAND

RL 4, 008–012

STANDING OUT
*A Bantam Skylark Book / January 1989*

*Sweet Valley High® and Sweet Valley Twins are
trademarks of Francine Pascal.*

*Conceived by Francine Pascal.*

*Cover art by James Mathewuse.*

*Produced by Daniel Weiss Associates, Inc.,
27 West 20th Street,
New York, NY 10011*

*Skylark Books is a registered trademark of Bantam Books,
a division of Bantam Doubleday Dell Publishing Group, Inc.
Registered in U.S. Patent and Trademark Office and elsewhere.*

*All rights reserved.*
*Copyright © 1988 by Francine Pascal.*
*No part of this book may be reproduced or transmitted
in any form or by any means, electronic or mechanical,
including photocopying, recording, or by any information
storage and retrieval system, without permission
in writing from the publisher.*
*For information address: Bantam Books.*

ISBN 0-553-15653-5

*Published simultaneously in the United States and Canada*

---

*Bantam Books are published by Bantam Books, a division of Bantam
Doubleday Dell Publishing Group, Inc. Its trademark, consisting of the
words "Bantam Books" and the portrayal of a rooster, is Registered in
U.S. Patent and Trademark Office and in other countries. Marca Regis-
trada. Bantam Books, 666 Fifth Avenue, New York, New York 10103.*

---

PRINTED IN THE UNITED STATES OF AMERICA

O     0 9 8 7 6 5 4 3 2 1

*To Sara Anne Weiss*

# One

◇

"Hey, Billie, wait up!" Jessica Wakefield called as Belinda Layton turned to leave the locker room after gym class.

"What's up, Jess?" Billie asked, slinging her red duffle bag over her shoulder. As usual, Billie's slender figure was hidden by the loose sweatpants and sweatshirt she always wore. Her light brown hair was pulled back in a pony-tail.

"I just wanted to tell you what a great job you did for our side," Jessica said breathlessly. Thanks to Billie's great dribbling and long throws, their team, the Stars, had defeated the Condors by eight points.

Billie looked pleased at Jessica's praise, but she didn't smile. "Thanks," she said sadly. "It's nice to know that somebody appreciates me."

Jessica tossed her long blond hair behind her shoulders and stared at Billie in disbelief. Had she just heard Billie Layton—all-around athlete, high-scorer on the basketball team, *and* star pitcher of the neighborhood Little League team, the Rangers—feeling sorry for herself?

"Of *course* people appreciate you," Jessica exclaimed. "How could they not?"

"Easily," Billie said.

"What's *wrong*, Billie?" Jessica demanded, pushing up the sleeves of her purple cardigan. "You've been acting so strange lately." Jessica had heard from someone on the Little League team that Billie had been sent home from baseball practice the day before. She'd struck out and thrown her bat over the fence in anger.

Billie's mouth turned down at the corners and Jessica thought she might cry.

"You'd act strange, too, Jessica, if your mom was having a baby," she blurted out.

"But that's great news, Billie!" Jessica exclaimed. "When is the baby due?"

"*You* may think it's great," Billie grumbled, beginning to walk away, "but *I* think it's awful. And it's due in just a few weeks, right in the middle of Little League season."

"But what's wrong with that?" Jessica asked, trying to match her shorter strides to Billie's longer, more powerful ones. "Babies are so cute! Imagine having your very own little sister or brother!" she added.

"It's a boy," Billie growled.

Jessica's blue-green eyes widened. "You mean, you already *know*?"

Billie nodded. "My mom's older than most mothers. So the doctor sent her to have a test to make sure the baby's healthy. That's how they found out it's a boy."

"Just think how *simple* that makes everything!" Jessica said excitedly. "You don't even have to worry about whether to buy pink or blue stuff for the baby's room."

"Yeah," Billie interrupted. "My dad put up the curtains Saturday afternoon. They've got these stupid little blue football players all over them." She scowled. "It's the first time my dad ever put curtains up."

Jessica giggled to herself. She had once seen Billie and her father out jogging together. He was a distinguished-looking ex-Navy commander who looked like he was standing at attention even in a sweatsuit. She couldn't imagine Commander Layton hanging baby curtains. "I guess he was trying to help your mom, huh?"

"I guess." Billie sighed. She looked straight at Jessica for the first time since they'd started to talk. "Listen, if you really don't mind hearing about it, I feel like I need to talk to someone— confidentially, I mean."

"It must be hard for you," Jessica sympathized. "I'm so lucky to have Elizabeth to listen to my problems."

Elizabeth was Jessica's identical twin and although they were different in many ways, they were closer than any two girls could be. They looked exactly alike with their long, silky blond hair, sparkling blue-green eyes, and dimples in their left cheeks. In fact, the only way to tell them apart was by their very different personalities.

Jessica was fun loving and always eager to gossip about boys, movie stars, and the latest fashions. She loved to be the center of attention in a large gathering of friends. Most of all, Jessica liked intrigue and high adventure which usually got her in a great deal of trouble.

Lucky for Jessica, Elizabeth was there most

of the time to bail her out of her messes. Older by four minutes, it often seemed more like four years. Like her sister, Elizabeth was fun loving, but she also had a serious side. She loved the time she spent talking with her closest friends, Amy and Julie, and the time she had alone to read a good mystery or do some writing.

*What a shame that Billie doesn't have someone as caring as Elizabeth to talk to,* reflected Jessica.

"Of course, there *is* Jim Sturbridge," Billie said, interrupting Jessica's thoughts. "Jim's my best friend. I can always count on him, and I can talk to him about *anything*." She bit her lip. "Except this. He'd think I was being a crybaby."

The bell that signaled the beginning of the lunch period almost drowned out her words, and kids began to spill out of the classrooms into the hall.

"Oh no!" Jessica moaned. "I'm sorry, Billie, but I've got to run. The Unicorns are having an emergency meeting at lunch, and I've just *got* to be there."

The Unicorn Club was an exclusive group who thought they were as special as the animal for which their club was named. They had adopted purple, the color of royalty, as their group color, and each day they tried to wear something purple. Elizabeth thought the Unicorn meetings were nothing more than gossip about boys and clothes. She also thought the girls in the club were snobs. Jessica loved being a Unicorn and took it all very seriously—especially emergency meetings. She put her hand on Billie's arm and flashed a wide smile. "Let's get together later, OK?"

Billie looked hurt, and Jessica, feeling a pang of guilt, thought that maybe she should skip the Unicorn meeting just this once. Then Billie's glum look disappeared when she spotted Jim Sturbridge walking past them down the crowded hall. "Hey, Jim!" she called, waving to him. But Jim didn't turn around. He was deep in conversation with a girl. "He must not have heard me," Billie muttered. "Well, see you later, Jessica." She walked away, looking a little disappointed.

Jessica couldn't help wondering why Jim was walking around with Sally Holcomb, one of the biggest flirts in the whole sixth grade, if he was *Billie's* best friend.

"This emergency meeting will come to order," Janet Howell, president of the Unicorn Club, commanded crisply. All the members stopped chattering and looked at Janet.

"Why are we having an emergency meeting?" Ellen Riteman asked, sounding worried.

"Don't tell me we're out of money again," Lila Fowler said with a weary sigh. The Unicorns were always overspending their budget for parties and dances, so fund-raisers were a constant topic of conversation.

Jessica smiled. Lila Fowler was one of her closest friends. Mr. Fowler was one of the wealthier men in Sweet Valley, and in Lila's mind, it was impossible to run out of money. She was used to getting anything she wanted.

"The problem can't be money," Mary Wallace reported confidently. "We've got sixteen dollars and thirty-two cents in the treasury."

"The problem *isn't* money," Janet said sternly. She leaned forward and lowered her voice so only the Unicorns could hear her. "The problem is image."

"Image?" Jessica asked, surprised. "How can there be anything wrong with our image?"

"Jessica's right, Janet," Lila said. She looked at all the members around her. "There isn't anybody here who doesn't fit the Unicorn image perfectly. Everyone here is both pretty *and* special."

The other Unicorns looked flattered, but Janet looked impatient. "You're all missing the point," she said. "Our image *is* our problem. People think we're stuck-up—that we're snobs."

Lila laughed and shrugged. "Well, of course that's what they think! They're jealous because *they're* not special enough to be Unicorns!" There was a general nod of agreement around the table.

"Actually, I wouldn't care about our image," Janet persisted, "if it weren't for the service award."

"What service award?" Mary asked.

"The one that's to be given next month to the organization that contributes the most to the community," Janet went on. "There's a prize that goes with the award." She paused, making sure that she had everyone's undivided attention. "The prize is an all-expense-paid, one-day trip for the whole organization—to the place of their choice within a fifty-mile radius."

Conversation buzzed around the table. Jessica sighed happily as she imagined the whole club taking a trip to a TV studio to see their favorite soap operas live. Or maybe they could all go to one of Johnny Buck's concerts! Johnny Buck was her favorite rock star.

Janet held up her hand for silence. "As I was saying," she went on, "if we want to win the service award, we will have to come across as helpful, rather than stuck-up. I want everybody to start thinking about ways to change our image," Janet continued. "We'll meet again in a few days, and I'd like everybody to have at least one suggestion. In the meantime, just practice being helpful—little things, like helping your teacher hand out papers, volunteering to be hall monitor, giving people directions. It's not all that hard, you know. And it could go a long way toward changing our image." With that, Janet took a sip of milk and turned her attention to her lunch. Then she cleared her throat and said, "Oh, and one more thing. It wouldn't be very good if word got out that we're worried about our image. So keep this confidential."

That evening, Elizabeth sat at her bedroom desk, typing a story for *The Sweet Valley Sixers*, the sixth-grade newspaper. Elizabeth was the editor and her hard work was largely responsible for its success.

"Hi, Lizzie!" Jessica bounced into the room and plopped down on the bed. "Got a minute?"

"Sure, Jess." Elizabeth sat back and stretched. She looked at the clock. "Fifty-nine," she said, counting seconds. "Fifty-eight, fifty-seven . . ."

Jessica giggled and tossed a pillow at her sister. "I mean, do you have a minute to *listen*, Big Sister? I need some advice."

Laughing, Elizabeth tossed the pillow back at Jessica. "Sure, I've got a minute," she said cheerfully. "What's up?"

"Well, it's about Billie Layton. She's pretty upset," Jessica said, leaning back against the pillows on the bed and tucking her feet under her. "I'm not supposed to repeat this, but since you're my twin, it's almost like telling myself."

Elizabeth wrinkled her brow. "Well, I'm not sure I understand what you just said, but go ahead."

"Did you know that Billie's mother is about to have a baby?" Jessica announced untucking one of her legs.

Elizabeth grinned. "Yes, I know. Don't you

remember when we were talking about Mrs. Layton at lunch the other day?" Billie's mother worked part-time in the school library. Then she frowned. "*That's* upsetting Billie? How come? It's so exciting! Being an only child must get kind of lonely sometimes."

For a second, Elizabeth tried to imagine how boring her life would be without Jessica or her older brother, Steven.

"She's getting a little brother," Jessica said, making figure eights with her foot. "They know that already."

"Well, maybe that's what's got her down," Elizabeth suggested. "I know she spends a lot of time with her father. And he comes to all of her ball games. Maybe she's afraid he won't have much time for her when the baby comes."

"But that's not the *problem*, Liz," Jessica said, sitting up. "The problem is Jim Sturbridge and Sally Holcomb," she added. "Billie says that Jim is her best friend, but I think maybe he means more than that to her. This morning we saw him walking with Sally Holcomb and Billie looked really upset." Jessica frowned. "Don't you think we should do something?"

"*We* should?" Elizabeth asked. Jessica had

an unsettling way of including her in her schemes. "Just what do you have in mind?" she asked suspiciously.

"Well, nothing, actually," Jessica said, waving her hand vaguely. "I just thought we could help somehow, that's all."

"It's nice that you want to help Billie," Elizabeth said, "but Jim has a right to be friendly with anybody he likes. It does sound as if Billie could use some cheering up."

Jessica stood up with a sigh. "I wish we could do something for her. Anyway, just remember not to tell anyone about this, OK?"

Elizabeth nodded, deep in thought. "The secret's safe with me," she said.

# *Two*

◇

"Hey, Billie, are you ready to go?" Jim Sturbridge asked, as Billie opened the door of her house on Tuesday morning.

"Yeah, I'm ready." Billie grabbed her books and called goodbye to her mother. She was glad that she and Jim were going to walk to school together. She wanted to discuss strategy for the big baseball game coming up on Saturday. They were scheduled to play the Rebels, their long-time rivals.

"So," Jim said, as they walked along, "are you all set for the game or do you need an extra workout or two?"

"Are you kidding?" Billie scoffed. "Hey, don't forget that this is the arm that wiped out the Cardinals last week." She whirled and threw an imaginary ball.

Jim looked serious. "Maybe so. But the Cardinals aren't good hitters. The Rebels are great hitters! Their first baseman is the top hitter in the league, and they've got a couple of other guys who are pretty good, too."

Billie cocked her head, feeling confident. "So what? I'll hold them to a couple of hits and you guys can get in there and score some big ones off their pitching." She grinned. "Piece of cake."

Jim laughed. "Boy, you sure make it sound easy, Billie." He put a friendly arm around her shoulders. "But there's no doubt about it, it's got to go that way. We can't win this game unless you can keep them from scoring." He dropped his arm. "We're counting on you."

Billie squared her shoulders. It felt good to know that he was relying on her. She wouldn't disappoint him.

There was something else that made her feel especially happy this morning. She and her father had had a talk the night before and had made plans to go fishing the day after the big game. In the old days, they'd gone fishing almost every weekend—just the two of them. But now with her mom's pregnancy, everything had changed and not for the better. Her mom hadn't felt well in the early months, so instead of going fishing with Billie on weekends, her dad had stayed around the house, helping her mother with the housework and other chores. Yet now that her mom was feeling better, he *still* stayed around the house, just to make sure that she had everything she needed—so he said. Billie suspected that he was worried about her mom, but even so, she felt left out. That's why the fishing trip was so special. Once the baby was born, Billie knew it would be a long time before she'd get to spend time alone with her dad again.

But what made Billie happiest of all was that during their talk, her father had promised to come to the big game on Saturday. This would give her a chance to show him how far she'd come since the last game he'd attended, weeks ago. She would put just the right spin on that super fastball he'd taught her. And then, after the game, they would sit down together and go over every play. It was too bad that her mother couldn't come, too, but she was so busy getting things ready for the baby. She hardly had time to think about anything else these days.

As Billie ambled down the sidewalk beside Jim, she decided she felt too good to dwell on any troubling matters—least of all, having seen Jim, the day before, with boy-crazy Sally Holcomb.

"Hand me those raisins, Jessica," Lila ordered, pushing her light brown hair out of her eyes. The girls were baking oatmeal cookies in Mrs. Gerhart's Tuesday morning home-ec class.

"Here you are," Jessica said.

Lila stirred the raisins into the dough. "And now the nuts."

Jessica handed Lila the nuts she'd just finished chopping. She and Lila were good friends, even though Lila could be bossy. Lila frequently insisted on doing the easy jobs, like mixing the dough, while her friends did the harder jobs, like chopping nuts.

"Now," Lila remarked, adding the nuts, "what was it you were saying about Billie Layton?"

"I was saying that Billie said Jim Sturbridge is her best friend," Jessica told her.

Lila began to drop little mounds of cookie dough onto the cookie sheet. "Well, if Jim

Sturbridge is Billie Layton's best friend," she said, "how come he's hanging around with Sally Holcomb? I saw the two of them having ice cream at Casey's Place the other day."

Jessica sighed and began to wash out the empty bowl Lila handed her.

Lila put the cookie sheet into the oven. "Somebody should tell Billie what's going on behind her back." She took off her apron and folded it up. "After all, Jessica, wouldn't *you* want to know if your boyfriend was sneaking around with some other girl? And while we're on the topic of Sally Holcomb, did you *see* that sweater she had on this morning? What gives her the right to wear a purple sweater? She's not a Unicorn!"

"Hi, Jessica."

Jessica whirled around and saw Elizabeth leaning on the counter next to her. Her sister had obviously finished making her cookies.

"Oh, hello, Elizabeth," Lila said smoothly. She rinsed her hands off in the sink, dried them, and then glanced at her watch. "Listen, Jessica, would you mind doing the rest of the dishes? I promised Mrs. Gerhart I'd talk to her the minute we were through."

Without waiting for Jessica's response, she added: "And I really think you ought to tell Billie about Jim and Sally. After all, it's not fair to keep her in the dark about something so important. Remember what Janet said about Unicorns being helpful? Well, this is a perfect opportunity." She picked up her books and walked toward the teacher's desk.

Elizabeth laughed. "I thought *you* were a whiz at getting out of the dishes, Jess, but Lila takes the grand prize." She gave her twin a sympathetic look. "Want me to help?"

Furious, Jessica reached for the dish towel. It was just like Lila to leave her with the dirty work. "Sure, thanks," she said gratefully. "If you'll wash, I'll dry."

Elizabeth ran water into the sink. "I thought you promised Billie not to talk about her problem, Jess."

"But I didn't mention the family stuff Billie told me about," Jessica countered. "Just the part about Jim Sturbridge, and then Lila brought up Sally Holcomb. Everyone but Billie knows about *them*."

Elizabeth turned to face her twin, her

hands covered with soapsuds. "You're not going to tell Billie, are you?" she asked.

Jessica dried the dish Elizabeth handed her. "Don't you think I should?"

"No!" Elizabeth snapped. "Jim and Billie are just friends, and what happens between Billie and Jim or Jim and Sally is entirely their own business. It's wrong to meddle or be a tattletale."

Jessica sighed and hung up the dish towel. "I guess you're right," she conceded.

Billie, still preoccupied by how much better things were, arrived at gym class a little late. Every girl had changed into her gym suit already and had lined up out on the floor—everyone except Jessica, who was standing in front of the locker-room mirror pulling her hair back.

"Hi, Billie," Jessica said. "I've been waiting for you. Maybe we can talk while you're getting ready."

Billie quickly opened her locker and pulled out her gym suit. "Oh, that's OK, Jessica," she said with a sheepish grin. "Everything's back to normal again—at least for now."

She took off her shoes and padded into one of the lavatory stalls. A clutch of panic seized her when she sat down. She had started her period—her very *first* period!

Billie sank down on the toilet lid. She'd studied all about menstruation in Health class, and her mother had explained it to her when she was younger, so this wasn't exactly a surprise. But still, she didn't feel prepared, and she certainly didn't have any of the things you needed.

"Billie, are you all right?" Jessica asked urgently, rapping on the door. "You've been in there a while."

Billie mustered up all of her courage. "Uh, Jessica," she said, nearly in a whisper, "do you happen to have any . . ." She swallowed. "I mean, uh, there's a machine on the wall by the door that sells . . . Could you put a quarter in it for me?"

"You mean," Jessica asked unbelievingly, "the machine by the *door*?" That was a machine that mostly seventh- and eighth-graders used.

"Yes," Billie said miserably. "That's the one I mean."

Jessica flew to get her purse and then

dashed to the machine. A moment later, she was back outside the stall again. "It's empty," she reported.

"It *can't* be," Billie moaned.

"Listen, don't move a muscle," Jessica commanded. "Lila and I share a gym locker and she keeps that stuff in there. It hasn't happened for her yet, but she says you have to think ahead about these things. I'll be right back."

Inside the stall, Billie fought back tears. *Don't move a muscle?* Where could she go? Just when she was thinking everything was back to normal, this had to happen.

In a jiffy, Jessica was back with a small box. "Here you are," she said, thrusting it through the door. "Do you need any help?"

"Thanks," Billie said glumly. "I think I can manage." But truthfully, she wasn't sure at all.

# *Three*

◇

A little while later, Billie was in the cafeteria having lunch with Jessica, Elizabeth, and Mary Wallace. She didn't have much of an appetite for the lasagna, though. Instead, she kept wondering which other girls in the cafeteria had gotten their periods. Her eye fell on Sally Holcomb, who was laughing and flirting with two boys. She didn't realize that she was staring until Jessica nudged her.

"Sally Holcomb is the boy-craziest girl in the whole sixth grade," Jessica said disgustedly. "Don't you think so?"

"Uh, I guess," Billie replied, flushing. She ducked her head, thinking about how shapely Sally was. Was *she* going to look like that in the next few months? What would happen when she tried to break her curveball over the plate?

Would her chest get in the way of her arm? And more horrible than that: Would she have to give up being a pitcher? The thought was so awful that Billie felt herself turning pale. Jessica patted her hand sympathetically, as if encouraging her to say what was on her mind.

But Billie didn't want to think about any of these disturbing matters any longer than she had to. She stood up and picked up her tray.

"I've got to go to music class," she said glumly. "I'll see you later."

Usually Billie enjoyed singing in music class, making her voice blend with the other voices, but today she had too much on her mind. She thought about Ms. McDonald, the new music teacher. Ms. McDonald had a well-developed figure, but she didn't seem to have any trouble using her arms, at least not that Billie could notice.

"Eyes up here, everybody," Ms. McDonald said, as she tapped on her music stand with her baton. "Now, let's try it once again, from the beginning."

Billie closed her eyes and tried to concentrate on her part, but all she could think about was class ending.

By the time her last class rolled around, Billie was tired of thinking about the changes in her body. She was ready to think about her schoolwork and nothing else, but when she walked into the classroom, she met Jessica and the rest of the class walking out, led by the vice principal, Mr. Edwards.

"Where's everybody going?" she asked, curious, falling into step with Jessica.

"To the library for a study hall," Jessica reported. "Ms. Wyler got called away and Mr. Edwards came in to tell us that they couldn't get a substitute on such short notice. And boy, am I glad!" she confided with a sigh of relief. "I didn't have my homework finished."

Billie nodded. She was happy, too. Now she'd get a chance to see her mom, who was working in the library this afternoon. What a lucky break!

Billie didn't spend as much time with her mother as she did with her dad, but today she could hardly wait to see her. She could tell her about getting her period and ask for some advice.

Mrs. Layton looked up from her desk in surprise when Mr. Edwards led the class into the library. He bent over and whispered something to her and then she stood up and came over to the tables where the class was sitting.

Billie blushed. Her mom looked awfully big, in spite of the loose top she was wearing. It was obvious that the baby was due very soon.

"Welcome, all of you, to your unscheduled library period," Mrs. Layton said with a warm smile. "If there are questions I can answer, or a book I can help you find, please let me know." She laughed. "Let's just hope it isn't on the bottom shelf," she added, and everybody giggled.

Billie stuck up her hand. Boy, did she have questions. "I'd like to talk to you," she said.

But Randy Mason, one of the smartest boys in the sixth grade, had beaten her to it. He was following her mother back to her desk with a long list of books in his hand. Billie watched as her mom spent almost fifteen minutes helping Randy.

Impatiently, Billie waited for her chance to approach her mother's desk and when it came she flew up front.

"Hello, Belinda," Mrs. Layton said cheerfully. "How's your day going?"

"Terrible," Billie groaned, pulling up a chair beside the desk. Her mother was the only one in the family who called her Belinda. "It's been just awful."

"Oh, I'm so sorry, honey," Mrs. Layton said sympathetically. "What happened?"

Billie looked around to make sure that nobody was within earshot, and then she leaned forward. "I was changing for gym this morning when I discovered—"

Julie Porter came around the bookshelf and stepped up to the desk. "Mrs. Layton, I have a question about a flute book." She looked at Billie. "Oh, hi, Billie," she said. "Listen, don't forget about my birthday party on Saturday. You *are* coming, aren't you?"

"Well, actually . . ." Billie began, a little embarrassed. She'd decided not to go to Julie's party, but she'd forgotten to tell her. The party was right after the big game, and since her father had promised to come, they'd probably stop off for ice cream afterward.

"A birthday party?" Mrs. Layton interrupted, smiling. "What fun! We'll have to see that you get a new party dress, Belinda! Something pretty and lacy, don't you think?"

A dress? Billie stared at her mother, alarmed. She didn't *need* a new party dress, especially one with lace on it. What she really needed—and before the game, too—was a new pair of sneakers.

"I know you've got a game on Saturday, Billie," Julie was saying, "but the party doesn't start until afterward, because most of the boys will be at the game. Just come whenever you get changed."

"Why, that sounds perfect, Belinda," Mrs. Layton said, getting slowly to her feet. "Now, let me help you find that book you're looking for, Julie."

Billie sighed dejectedly. "I guess we can't talk now, Mom," she said.

Mrs. Layton smiled down at her. "We can have the whole evening together if you want, honey. Right now I have to help Julie."

Billie trudged back to the table and put her head down on her arm. Didn't her mother even care about her? Everybody seemed more important than she did. First there was the baby, disrupting the family and taking everybody's attention, and now her mother didn't have time to talk to her because she had to answer all the other kids' questions. Nobody seemed to have time for Billie.

It just wasn't *fair*!

# *Four*

◇

After school on Tuesday, Elizabeth and Billie waited for Jessica in front of the school.

"Hi, Jessica," Elizabeth called when she spotted Lila and Jessica coming down the front steps. "Over here." She and Jessica had made a date to go to Billie's house in the hope of cheering up their friend.

"Hi," Jessica said, as she and Lila joined Elizabeth and Billie.

"Are you ready to go to Billie's?" Elizabeth asked eagerly.

"Oh, no!" Jessica's hand flew to her mouth. "Gosh, Billie, I forgot all about . . . that is, the Unicorns are meeting this afternoon at Janet's house to talk about something really important. I mean, it's *crucial*. There's no way I can miss it."

"That's right," Lila chimed in. "It's crucial."

At that moment, Aaron Dallas, one of Billie's Ranger teammates, came along, and Billie started talking to him about the upcoming game. While she was occupied, Elizabeth leaned toward her twin. "But we *promised* we'd spend this afternoon with Billie," she whispered. "Don't forget, you're the one who wanted to do something to help cheer her up."

"And I still do," Jessica whispered back, with a stricken look. "I really want to help! It's just that—"

"Jessica," Lila interrupted abruptly, "if we're going to get to the meeting on time, we'd better go. You know how Janet feels about people being late."

Jessica gulped. "I'm coming," she said hastily, as Lila started to walk away. "Billie," she added, "I'm really sorry about today. I'll come over to your house one day soon, OK?" She turned and dashed off after Lila.

"I apologize for Jessica," Elizabeth said soberly, as they started walking home. "Sometimes she has a little trouble remembering all the plans she's made."

"That's OK, Elizabeth," Billie said with a sigh. "Sometimes it's hard to keep track of everything." She paused. "Especially when things happen so fast."

"Are things changing that quickly with you, too?" Elizabeth asked gently.

Billie gave a little laugh. "Boy, you can say that again. Changes, changes, and more changes. And none that I'd exactly wish for. I got my period today in gym class," she confided, staring at her feet.

"You did?" Elizabeth exclaimed. "Wow, that's great!"

"Yeah, I guess it is," Billie said. "It's just that there are so *many* changes in my life right now, I didn't quite feel ready for another one." She kicked at a stone on the sidewalk. "I've been trying to tell my mom, but these days she's either too busy or too tired."

Before the girls realized it, they were at Billie's house. On their way in, they stopped in the kitchen to grab some snacks and then headed directly up the stairs to Billie's room.

"Welcome," Billie said with mock formality, as she ushered Elizabeth into her bedroom.

Elizabeth looked around and grinned. The neat, sunny room was *exactly* like Billie. The yellow-and-white walls were decorated with baseball pennants and posters of sports heroes, and a fishing rod leaned against a wall in the corner. Piled up in the opposite corner were a pitcher's glove, a baseball, some bats and a red batting helmet. An autographed football sat on her desk.

"The football belonged to my dad when he was at the Naval Academy," Billie said proudly, picking it up for Elizabeth to get a closer look. "It's my most valued possession."

"So your dad is into sports, too," Elizabeth commented, as Billie opened one of the sodas they'd brought up.

"He's taught me everything I know," Billie said simply. "Sometimes I think he was disappointed I wasn't a boy. But it didn't stop him from teaching me everything he would have taught a boy to do. We used to do everything together. But—"

"But what?" Elizabeth prompted softly.

"But we don't do many things together anymore," she said sadly, burying her face in her arms.

"If you ask me," Lila commented tartly, as the Unicorns were settled into the den at Janet

Howell's house, "this whole thing is a lot of nonsense."

"I don't see how you can say that, Lila," Janet replied, raising her chin. "You can't deny that the Unicorns have an image problem."

"It all depends," she said, fingering the unicorn charm that hung on a gold chain around her neck, "on your definition of an image problem." She smiled at the others. "Personally, I like our image just the way it is."

"Me, too!" Ellen Riteman agreed.

"Well, I think Janet's right," Mary Wallace said quietly. "The Unicorns *are* special, and that's good—for us. But lots of kids feel left out because they can't belong. If we could include them in some of the things we do, it might change the way they look at us."

"Include other people in our club?" Ellen asked in horrified disbelief. "You mean, girls who *aren't* Unicorns? People like Lois Waller?" Lois was the chubbiest girl in the sixth-grade class.

At the mention of the girl's name, everybody giggled. When they all quieted down Jessica turned to Mary.

"Go on, Mary," she said encouragingly. "What kind of plan did you have in mind?"

"Well, it's not a plan, exactly. And I wasn't suggesting that we bring other people into the club. I was thinking that maybe the Unicorns could start a tutoring service." She looked around the table. "After all, a lot of us have pretty good grades. And there are lots of kids who need help after school. We could meet in the library and—"

Lila Fowler shrugged. "Well, I for one have *no interest* in tutoring students after school," she said firmly. "In the library or anywhere else."

"Well, then," Jessica volunteered, "how about running errands for sick people?" The idea had just popped into her head. For a moment she imagined herself with a basket, buying bread for a little old lady with a broken hip or a sore throat. Maybe she'd even bump into Tom McKay or Colin Harmon, the cutest boys at school, who'd offer to help her with the errands.

Kimberly Haver frowned. "But how would we find out who the sick people are?" she asked. "Would we just knock on doors and say, 'Pardon me, but are there any sick people here I can run an errand for?'"

Everybody laughed and Jessica sat back, wishing she hadn't volunteered her idea.

"It's clear that this matter requires more discussion," Janet said. "Mary's and Jessica's ideas are both good, but we ought to have some other suggestions to consider, too."

Lila pushed her chair back. "Well, my suggestion is that we table this idea for now and talk about more important things, like Julie Porter's birthday party." She looked around the table. "I've got a fabulous new dress, with purple velvet ribbons on it. What are the rest of you going to wear?"

"Gosh," Elizabeth exclaimed, looking at her watch. "It's after five o'clock. I've got to get home and help my mom with supper."

Billie got up from the floor and stretched. They'd talked for a while and then decided to play Scrabble. The game had been close, but Elizabeth had finally beaten her.

"Belinda?" Billie could hear her mother calling from downstairs. "Belinda, we're home."

"I'm up here, Mom," Billie called. "My dad took my mom to the doctor this afternoon for a checkup," she explained to Elizabeth.

Elizabeth finished putting away the tiles. "I hope everything's OK."

"Oh, it is," Billie said. She took the box Elizabeth handed her and put it on the closet shelf. "Thanks for coming over," she said. "Too bad Jessica couldn't make it."

Elizabeth didn't say anything. She was looking at the clothes in Billie's closet. Then she turned to Billie. "Listen," she said, "speaking of Jessica, the two of us are planning to go shopping on Thursday, over at the mall. Jessica wants to get something new for Julie's party. Would you like to come along?"

"Shopping?" Billie asked, screwing up her face. "I was going to go to the park after school on Thursday to practice for Saturday's game." Then she remembered her mother's idea about buying her a new dress for the party. Maybe she should go shopping with the twins in order to pick out her own dress, and maybe she could even get those sneakers she needed, too.

"On second thought," she added, "that's not such a bad idea."

"Terrific!" Elizabeth exclaimed happily. "Mom can pick us up and drive us to the mall right after school. I'll tell Jessica you're coming. She'll really be glad."

Billie walked Elizabeth downstairs and said

goodbye to her at the front door. Then she wandered down the hall in the direction of the kitchen, where she could hear the faint murmur of her parents' voices.

Billie didn't mean to eavesdrop, but when she got near the kitchen door, she heard her father say, "The doctor's report we got today was super, Margaret. It won't be long now."

"No, it won't," her mother said. "In fact, I think it's time to decide on a name." Billie heard her mother sigh. "I think you're right, David. We ought to name the baby William Arthur, after your father."

Outside the door, Billie leaned against the jamb and sucked in her breath sharply. *William?* They were going to name the baby *William?*

"Are you sure, Margaret?" her father asked. "It's bound to cause Belinda difficulties. After all, we've been calling her Billie—" He paused and corrected himself. "—*I've* been calling her Billie for almost twelve years now. She might feel like we're taking something away from her—something that *belongs* to her."

"I know," her mother said. "She may be a little upset when we tell her, but I think she's mature enough to understand why it's so important that we name her brother after her grandfather."

"Right," her father agreed. His voice dropped a little, and Billie could almost hear her heart pounding. "Now we've got a boy to carry it on. My father would be so proud."

Billie swallowed. Her name. They were taking her name away from her. And then, shoulders sagging, tears blurring her eyes, Billie turned and ran upstairs.

# Five

◇

"Elizabeth!" Jessica poked her head out of her door and into the upstairs hall as Elizabeth walked by. "Could you come here for a minute?"

"What's up?" Elizabeth asked. "What do you want to borrow now?" The minute she entered her sister's room, she shrieked in mock horror. "Jess! What's happened to your *room*?"

Jessica looked around her neat, spotless room, and said proudly, "It does look rather nice, doesn't it?" She had picked up all her clothes and magazines and record albums, and she'd straightened her shelves. She'd even vacuumed the cookie crumbs off the rug and taken all the dirty dishes down to the kitchen.

"I don't believe it," Elizabeth said, stunned. She shook her head and took another look around the room. "I can *walk* without tripping over something! And look! There's your bed!"

"Very funny, Elizabeth," Jessica said. It was true she wasn't usually very neat but she thought Elizabeth was exaggerating just a bit.

Elizabeth gingerly approached the closet.

"I'll bet," she said, "that your closest is so full that . . ." She slid the door open and jumped back, as if to escape an avalanche. To her surprise, nothing happened. Cautiously she stuck her head inside and then moved back out. She came over to the bed and put her hand anxiously to Jessica's forehead.

"You're not sick or anything, are you Jess?" she asked. "Should we call a doctor? An ambulance? Where did you put everything? Your room hasn't looked like this since the day you moved into it."

Jessica tried to suppress her giggles but soon both girls roared with laughter.

"Well, Jess," Elizabeth said at last, looking around. "Congratulations. This is *certainly* a new you."

"It is?" Jessica asked, wide-eyed. "Do you really think so?" She was about to tell Elizabeth that cleaning her room actually was part of a campaign to change her image when she remembered the strict orders not to discuss the Unicorns' plan with *anybody*.

Instead she said, "Speaking of changes, how was Billie today?" She had meant to ask Elizabeth about Billie at dinner, but the Wakefields had had company and she hadn't gotten a chance.

Elizabeth sat down on Jessica's bed and folded her legs under her. "She seemed a little down, especially after her mom and dad got home from the doctor. It's too bad you couldn't have been there, Jess."

"I know," Jessica said sadly. "I would have come, but the Unicorns would have been angry if I'd missed the meeting. I've been thinking about Billie a lot, though, and I know that we just *have* to help her."

"We already are helping her," Elizabeth pointed out. "What she needs is friends she can talk to, do things with. In fact, she's agreed to go shopping with us on Thursday."

"Well, that's good. But that's not what I meant. I meant that we have to help her about this Jim-and-Sally business." Jessica laid her hand on her sister's arm and said in her most serious tone, "I know what you're thinking, Lizzie, but I'm not doing this to be a tattletale. I really want to help Billie. And I've got an idea. All we have to do is write a letter."

Elizabeth sat up straight. "A letter?"

"Yes. You can type it so she won't recognize the handwriting. Just say that Jim is hanging around with Sally. That's all," she said. "Just the truth."

Elizabeth folded her arms over her chest. "I refuse," she said firmly, shutting her eyes. "I positively, absolutely, and for the last time *refuse* to have anything to do with this nasty scheme of yours."

"But we have to help her!" Jessica wailed. "How about this? We could find out when Jim and Sally are going to be together, and then we could lure Billie there so she could see with her own eyes what's going on behind her back. That way, we'll be showing her, not telling her! She really should know that she can't count on Jim Sturbridge."

Elizabeth stood up. "Jessica," she said, in a threatening voice.

"Or," Jessica said pleadingly, "maybe I

could plant something in *The Sweet Valley Sixers* gossip column. You know, just a little clue. Like, 'Guess who we saw walking down the hall together, *again*.' And all you have to do is OK the column."

Elizabeth turned and strode to the door. "Jessica, the best way for you to help Billie Layton is to go shopping with us on Thursday and help her buy something really pretty to wear to Julie's party." She paused, and a reflective note crept into her voice. "When I was over there today, I looked in her closet, and you know what?"

"What?" Jessica asked, pouting.

"There wasn't one single dress in her closet."

"Wow!" Jessica said in a whisper.

"That's why, on Thursday, *we* are going to help Billie buy herself a dress."

Jessica was quiet for a moment. Why, of course! Why hadn't she thought of it sooner? First they would help Billie buy a dress, and then they'd give her a complete makeover. By the end of the party Jim Sturbridge would be knocked right off his feet. And Billie, herself, even though she was sort of a tomboy, would be able to see that being a girl was pretty neat after all. It was a wonderful plan!

"Oh, Lizzie!" Jessica cried, jumping up and down. "You have the best ideas in the whole world!"

After school on Wednesday, Billie rushed home to change into her Rangers uniform. She loved baseball practice, but even more she loved her walks home with Jim afterward. She quickly slipped into her uniform, pulled her hair back, and shoved on her Rangers cap. Then, grabbing her glove and her batting helmet, she raced to the park as fast as she could.

When Billie arrived, Jim Sturbridge and the other guys were already in batting practice and there were a dozen or so parents in the bleachers. Billie smiled as she approached the field and heard the crack of the bat against the ball. It was a sound she loved—as long as it wasn't *her* pitch that got hit!

Coach Andrews raised his arms and motioned the team over to the bench. "OK, everybody," he began. "Today's a scrimmage game so we're going to rotate. Everyone will get a chance at the plate." He raised his voice. "OK, gang, let's see your stuff!"

The team ran out on the field and Coach Andrews turned to Billie. "How's your arm today, kid?"

"Fine, Coach," she answered enthusiastically. "Never been better."

"Then take the mound. And don't forget, you're starting on Saturday."

He didn't have to remind her. Of course she was starting on Saturday! Who else had a fastball as good as hers? She was the only one who could keep the Rebels from hitting.

Billie trotted out to the mound and turned to face Aaron Dallas. Suddenly she began to feel painfully self-conscious. For the first time, she noticed that all the other players on the team were *boys*. Billie wondered if there was any way that the guys could possibly know that she had gotten her period.

Instantly, her mouth felt dust-dry and her breath was coming hard. When she wound up for the special overhand delivery her father had taught her, something unexpected happened. The ball sailed over the plate, fast and low, right where Aaron liked it, and he put his bat squarely on it. With a hard, clean *swoosh*, the ball sailed over the center fielder's head and smacked the fence in the farthest corner of the park.

"Hey, thanks, Billie," Aaron called, giving her the thumbs-up sign as he trotted from second to third. He was safely home long before the throw came from second base.

Billie managed to strike out the second batter, but when the count was three balls and two strikes on the third batter, Jim snatched off his face mask and trotted out to the mound for a conference.

"What's up, Billie?" he asked in a worried voice. "You coming down with something?"

Billie looked down at the ground. "Just give me a minute, huh? I'm still getting warmed up."

"You've had a minute," Jim pointed out. "This is the third batter, and your curveball hasn't broken right once."

"Don't worry," Billie said, her voice rising in spite of her efforts to stay calm.

"OK, OK," Jim muttered. "Don't get all shook up." He walked back to the plate, shaking his head.

Billie did break it, finally. She threw some nice curveballs, but she still wasn't throwing with her usual spark. When the inning was over, Billie trotted off the field, wondering whether her period had anything to do with the way she had pitched today.

Coach Andrews didn't help matters. "Billie," he said, motioning her over to the bench while the others packed up their gear, "looks like you were having a little trouble out there."

Billie shrugged. "It came out OK," she said defensively. "I got those last three batters, didn't I?"

"Sure, you did," the coach said, putting a friendly hand on her shoulder. "And it'll come out all right on Saturday, too. You just have to loosen up a little and give that fastball more steam."

Coach Andrews gave her bicep a critical squeeze. "You need some more muscle behind that ball. Maybe it'd help if you'd try a little weight lifting at home. Get your dad to show you how."

Without a word, Billie turned and walked away. *Weight lifting?* Was he saying that her fastball wasn't working anymore? Furiously, she slammed her glove on the ground.

"Hey, Billie, see you tomorrow at school," Jim called to her as he was leaving.

"Wait!" Billie scooped up her glove and ran to catch up with him. "Aren't we walking home together?"

"Sorry, I can't today," Jim said. "I've got something I have to do. See you tomorrow, OK?"

"Sure," Billie said, trying to hide her disappointment. She turned and walked away. A dull, unhappy feeling settled in the pit of her stomach. Was it because the coach had questioned her pitching ability or was it because she didn't get to walk home with Jim?

She was so busy with her thoughts that she almost didn't see Sally Holcomb hurrying down the other side of the street toward the ballpark. But when Billie looked up and spotted her—she felt even worse.

# Six

◇

After school on Thursday, Mrs. Wakefield dropped Elizabeth, Jessica, and Billie off outside of Valley Fashions, a shop in the mall that specialized in teen and preteen clothing. Billie felt a little uncomfortable. She wasn't used to shopping for dresses.

Jessica didn't seem to be having any difficulty, though. "Wow," she said happily. "Look at all the new sweaters they got in!"

"But we're not here to buy sweaters," Elizabeth reminded her. "We're here to buy dresses for Julie's party—all three of us."

"I know," Jessica sighed. "But that doesn't mean I can't look, does it?" She wandered off, humming happily to herself.

Elizabeth turned to Billie with a grin. "When she comes back, she'll have half a dozen outfits over her arm. Choosing one of them will take at least a half hour. Why don't we get started? What did you have in mind?"

Billie bit her lip. Some skirts on a rack caught her eye. "Well," she said slowly, "maybe I could get a blue denim skirt and—"

"I don't think blue denim is quite right for this party," Elizabeth said. She went over to a dress rack and picked out a pink dress with ruffles at the neck and sleeves.

Billie watched Elizabeth with horror. She hated pink. And ruffles. "No," she said quickly. "That's not what I want."

Elizabeth pulled something else off the rack, a white dress with a full skirt. "How about this?" she asked.

Billie shook her head. "It's pretty, but I'd get it dirty too quickly. With my luck, I'd spill chocolate on it."

In the end, Billie found a pretty blue dress with a tiny flower print. She didn't mind that it had a narrow lace collar, because the lace was soft, not starchy or prickly. And the blue velvet ribbon that looped around the waist was a nice touch. She looked at the dress and suddenly found herself wondering whether Jim would like it. Then she shook her head at the thought. What a dumb thing to wonder. She turned back to the rack and took another dress, dark blue and very plain, with narrow sleeves and a high collar.

"Have you found something, Billie?" Jessica asked, coming over with her arms full of clothes. "Why don't we all go into the dressing room together?"

Hesitantly, Billie followed the girls as they searched for a dressing room big enough for all three of them. Jessica insisted on being first, while Elizabeth and Billie watched her model different outfits, one at a time.

"Well," she said, turning around in front of the mirror, wearing the last one, "which do you like?"

"Definitely the pink-and-white," Elizabeth said. "It's you." Billie nodded. "The pink looks nice on you," she said.

Then it was Billie's turn. Self-consciously, she slipped into the first blue dress she had chosen.

"Wait, Billie," Jessica objected impatiently.

"You can't tell much about a dress if you leave your jeans on under it!"

With an embarrassed giggle, Billie shed her jeans, too. Then she stood in front of the mirror, not looking at her reflection, while Jessica zipped the dress up the back and Elizabeth tied the blue velvet ribbon at the waist.

Jessica nodded in satisfaction. "This is the one," she said. "It's perfect."

Billie looked in the mirror. It didn't look at all like *her*. The image was all wrong and it made her uncomfortable.

"I think I'd better try on the other dress," she said slowly, turning her back to the mirror. "The dark blue one. I think I like it better."

"Oh, no!" Jessica exclaimed. "This one looks great on you, Billie. Don't you think so, Elizabeth? Why, it'll make Ji—" She put her hand over her mouth. "It'll make every boy at the party look at you!"

Elizabeth's eyes bore through her sister, but Billie didn't notice. She wasn't at all sure she liked the idea of *every* boy looking at her—unless they were admiring her fastball, that is. She turned around in front of the mirror, and the thought of Jim crept back into her mind. If she had barely recognized herself, what would Jim say when he saw her all dressed up? The thought made her cheeks flush pink.

"I agree with Jessica," Elizabeth said, and that settled it. Jessica and Billie paid for their purchases and the three girls stopped in the shoe store next door so Billie could buy a pair of sneakers.

"Wait, Billie," Jessica said, as the shoe salesman was headed for the cash register. "Don't you need a pair of shoes to go with your dress?" She sat down beside Billie and handed her a pair. "These would be perfect with it."

Billie looked at the shoes. They were shiny white with a strap. They *were* very nice. She tried to imagine how they would look with the dress, but then she pushed the thought out of her mind. "I don't need party shoes," she objected. "I've got a perfectly good pair of school shoes I can wear."

Elizabeth turned to face Billie. "Do you have enough money with you?" she whispered.

Billie nodded. Her mother had given her more than enough.

"Well, then," Elizabeth said, "I vote for the shoes. They're really pretty. And they do go with the dress."

So in the end, Billie bought two pairs of shoes after all—the sneakers for the game and the white ones for the party.

As they walked out into the mall, Elizabeth looked at her watch. "Mom said she'd pick us up out front at five," she said. "We'd better hurry."

Billie followed along happily. Shopping with the twins had been much more fun than she had expected. "Listen, Billie," Jessica was saying. "I've got a great idea. Why don't you come home with us after the game on Saturday and we'll all get dressed for the party together?"

"That's a terrific plan, Jess," Elizabeth agreed.

Billie hesitated. "Well, I don't know. My father promised to come to the game and we might go for ice cream or something afterward. He always critiques my game."

"You can talk to him later about the game. This way, we can all go to the party together," Elizabeth said determinedly.

"I guess you're right," Billie said. The more

she thought about it, the better the idea seemed. After all, she might feel a little funny walking into the party all by herself. It would definitely be better to arrive with the twins.

"Great!" Jessica exclaimed. "We'll have a get-ready-for-the-party party!"

Billie giggled along with Jessica. The twins were turning out to be pretty great friends.

Just then, they rounded a corner in the mall. Billie looked up and her heart sank to the pit of her stomach. Coming out of Casey's Place, directly in front of them, was Jim Sturbridge. And hanging onto his arm and laughing flirtatiously, was Sally Holcomb!

Billie couldn't believe what she saw. Jim— with Sally! Then the truth hit her. Sally had come to the ballpark the day before to meet Jim. That was the reason he couldn't walk home with her. He'd made plans to be with Sally! Then she remembered seeing them together in the hallway the week before. Suddenly, it was all very clear, and Billie felt sick.

From the look on Jim's face, it was obvious that he wasn't too happy about bumping into Billie, either. The only happy face was Sally's as she clung to Jim's arm.

"Hi, Jessica," she cooed sweetly. "Hi, Elizabeth." Her glance swiveled to Billie and her voice became a little cooler. "Hello, Billie."

Jessica and Elizabeth returned her greeting. But Billie mumbled a barely audible hello. Jim was too embarrassed to say anything.

"Jim," Sally said giving him a little nudge, "we have to go. See you guys later, OK?"

The three girls just watched as Jim and Sally walked away.

"I'm really sorry," Jessica said quietly, with a sympathetic glance at Billie. "I wanted to tell you about Jim and Sally, but—"

"It's OK," Billie cut in. "I guess I'm just as glad I didn't know." She looked down at the shopping bags she was carrying and started to walk toward the exit. The whole idea of the blue dress seemed very silly now.

Once outside the mall, Billie took a deep breath and tried desperately to push down the misery that was welling up inside her. But she just couldn't hold it in any longer.

"Why couldn't things go on the way they were?" she burst out suddenly. "Why did everything in my life have to change?" She made her way to a nearby bench and plopped down disgustedly.

"I guess," Elizabeth said quietly, sitting down beside her, "that that's the way life is."

"Yes," Jessica added. "Remember what Mr. Nydick said about the dinosaurs? He said the reason they all became extinct was because they couldn't adapt. Well, I guess we have to adapt."

Just at that moment, the Wakefields' maroon van pulled up at the curb and the three girls climbed in. Elizabeth and Jessica tried to make conversation, but Billie was silent all the way home. When they got to the end of Billie's block, she leaned forward. "Could you let me out here, Mrs. Wakefield?" she asked. "There's something I want to do."

"But your house is at the other end of the street," Elizabeth objected.

"That's OK," Billie said. "I feel like walking."

Mrs. Wakefield pulled over to the curb and Billie hopped out. "Thanks for helping me pick out a dress," she said to Jessica and Elizabeth before shutting the car door.

"Are you sure you don't want us to walk with you?" Elizabeth asked anxiously. Billie looked so sad.

"Thanks, but I need some time to be alone." Billie closed the door gently and started down the block.

"I don't understand," Mrs. Wakefield said. "Did something happen at the mall? Did you girls have a disagreement?"

"No," Jessica said, with a worried look. "Billie just found out the truth about someone, that's all."

It was almost five-thirty, but the sun was still above the horizon. Angrily, Billie wiped the tears from her eyes. It was silly to cry over Jim Sturbridge! she told herself. She was going to stop it this instant. She cut across a vacant lot down the block from her house, and then, on an impulse, took the overgrown path that led down to the creek. When she reached it, she sat down on the familiar willow stump and stared down into the dark water. Then she broke into uncontrollable sobs.

For the next five minutes, she just cried hopelessly. She cried because everything familiar and certain was changing. There was nobody left in the world whom she could count on anymore.

Behind her there was a rustle in the grass, and Billie turned to see her mother making her way slowly down the path. She quickly looked back at the water and rubbed the tears off her cheeks with the back of her hand.

"I saw you heading down here," her mother said, leaning against the willow behind Billie. She was out of breath from climbing down the path. "Is everything all right?"

Billie sat numbly. Now was the time to talk to her mother about getting her period, about her poor performance on the pitcher's mound yesterday. She could even tell her about Jim and Sally, and how hopeless she felt about everything. But as much as she longed to break the silence, she couldn't.

"I know," her mother said softly. "Sometimes there's just too much to tell, isn't there, honey? It all must feel overwhelming." She put her hands lightly on Billie's shoulders and then leaned over and hugged her.

Billie was glad her mother didn't insist that she talk. She gave her mother a big hug. Then she stood up, took her mother's hand, and together they walked back home in silence.

# Seven

◇

Saturday finally arrived. Billie went to the ballpark early to warm up. She felt tense and jittery. There was so much riding on this game. Her father was going to be here, and she wanted to shine for him. Jessica had told her that she and Elizabeth and several of their friends would be in the stands, cheering for her, and she didn't want to disappoint them either. Of course she had to show Jim Sturbridge and Sally Holcomb that she didn't care *what* they did! But most of all, Billie wanted to prove that all these changes weren't going to affect the way she played baseball.

In spite of the pep talk she gave herself, the pre-game warm-up wasn't very promising. Her arm felt stiff and the ball seemed to have a mind of its own, skittering into the dust or sailing wildly over Jim's head.

Since it was a home game, the Rangers took the field first and the Rebels, their opponents, were first up to bat. Out on the mound, digging her new sneakers into the dirt to loosen them up a little, Billie scanned the packed bleachers. She caught a glimpse of Sally in the second row, and quickly looked away. She searched the stands for her father but couldn't spot him. Was he going to be late, she wondered, on this all-important day? Then she saw Jessica, Elizabeth, and their friends, sitting together on the highest row, waving pom-poms and chanting her name. This made her feel a little better. It was nice to have her own cheering section.

Once the game started, though, Billie began to wish Jessica and the others hadn't come. There wasn't very much to cheer about. She managed to get the first batter to foul-tip the ball to Jim behind the plate for an automatic out. But the second batter hit a sizzling line drive off her curveball. Luckily, the shortstop got a glove on it and threw the batter out at first. Two outs. But then, the sky darkened and thunder growled and she *walked* the next two batters!

Jim made a time-out sign to the umpire and trudged out to the mound. "So what do you think?" he asked casually, not really looking at her. "Think you can get this next guy?"

"Sure, no problem," Billie said, trying to keep the nervousness out of her voice.

Jim met her eyes. For a moment he didn't say anything. Then he asked, "How about a fastball, then? Catch the outside corner, maybe. And a little high?"

Billie nodded. "Outside, high," she repeated. "Gotcha."

Jim grinned. "Go get him!" He turned and trotted back. Behind Billie, the runner on second began to chant. "How about a hit! Let's have a hit!" In the stands, Jessica and her friends were jumping up and down, flinging their pom-poms into the air. "Come on, Billie!" they screamed. "Get him out!"

Pumping hard, her eyes fixed on the plate, Billie began her windup. High and outside, Jim had said, and that's what she aimed for. But the second the ball left her fingers, she knew it was low. Low and across the middle of the plate. The batter connected with it solidly—a smoking line drive flew past her and smashed into the right-field fence. Billie turned to watch, her heart

sinking right down into the toes of her brand-
new sneakers. It was an easy triple.

The two Rebels already on base scored
runs, their fans cheering wildly. The batter raced
toward third and sensing a chance for a home
run, poured on the speed, heading for the plate.

The right fielder's throw came at Billie. She
caught the ball, whirled and threw as hard as
she could, aiming for the mitt Jim held out as
he crouched on top of home plate. Her throw got
to the plate a split second before the runner did.

"Out!" the umpire yelled, jerking his
thumb over his shoulder. The Ranger fans went
crazy, shouting her name louder than ever.

Billie was relieved for a moment as she trotted back to the bench, but she knew she was still
in trouble. She had been lucky to get out of that
jam with only two runs—not exactly a great performance. She'd have to do better than that in
the next inning. The rest of the Rangers didn't
seem worried, though. Batting well, they scored
two runs in their half of the inning, much to the
fans' delight.

When Billie took the field again for the top
of the second, she was *glad* that her father

hadn't come yet. The game was tied at two-all and Dennis Cookman, the team's relief pitcher was warming up along the first-base line. She walked the first batter. The second batter slammed the ball deep into center field for a double. The great pitching arm that Billie could always depend on had failed her completely. The people in the stands stirred uneasily. Even Jessica and the others were silent. And now it was starting to drizzle.

As Billie turned back to the plate to face the third batter, she saw Jim take his face mask off. On the sidelines, Coach Andrews stood up from the bench and motioned for time out. He gestured to Dennis to take his place on the pitcher's mound.

Billie's shoulders slumped and she blinked away the tears. She was being pulled from the game.

It was all over.

# *Eight*

◇

It was raining harder now. Big drops splattered on the wooden bleachers noisily. Elizabeth opened her yellow umbrella and Jessica joined her beneath it.

"What's happening down there, Liz?" Jessica asked in a worried voice.

"It looks like they're bringing in a relief pitcher," Elizabeth said sadly, as Billie walked toward the bench.

"Does that mean Billie's finished?" Amy Sutton asked, pushing her damp hair out of her eyes. "Aren't they going to give her another chance?" Amy was one of Elizabeth's closest friends.

"It looks like she's through for today," Elizabeth replied, watching Billie pull her cap off.

"This is a *dumb* game," Lila said. "There's

no excitement at all." She pulled the hood of her red raincoat over her head and frowned up at the dark sky.

Suddenly a big clap of thunder crashed across the sky and everybody jumped.

"That's it," Lila announced, standing up. "I'm not hanging around here to get rained on. I don't want my hair to be all stringy for Julie's party."

"Me, either," Ellen agreed, and all the other girls began to gather their things.

Amy looked at Elizabeth. "Are you leaving?" she asked.

Elizabeth shook her head. How would Billie feel if she looked up into the bleachers and saw that everybody had gone? "I've got an umbrella," she said. She grinned at Amy. "There's room for three under it," she added. Eagerly, Amy moved in toward Elizabeth's other side.

Lila stuck her nose up in the air. "Come on, Jessica," she ordered. "The *Unicorns* are leaving."

Elizabeth glanced at her sister. When Lila used that tone of voice, Jessica always gave in. But not today. Jessica looked up at Lila and said firmly, "You guys can go. I'm staying."

"But Jessica—" Ellen began.

Lila stopped her. "Jessica can stay if she wants to," she said haughtily. "I don't have the time to argue with her." With a loud harrumph, she marched down the bleacher steps, leading the others away.

Elizabeth reached for Jessica's hand and gave it a happy squeeze. "Thanks, Jess," she said.

Jessica looked up. "Do you think I could have a little more of that umbrella? It's wet on this side."

Amy pointed down below, where a small overhang off to the side sheltered part of one bench. "Maybe we could move down there," she suggested. "It might be drier."

"Good idea," Jessica said, and they all scuttled down to the second row.

Down on the bench, Billie glanced up toward the bleachers for the third or fourth time. Her father still wasn't there. With a sharp pang she realized that he must have changed his mind about coming after all. She wasn't sure whether to be glad that he hadn't witnessed her humiliation or to be angry that he had failed to keep his promise.

Then, out of the corner of her eye, she saw Sally Holcomb making her way down the bleachers. Jessica, Elizabeth, and Amy Sutton were leaving their seats.

Gloomily, Billie turned her attention to the field again. She couldn't count on *anybody*, she thought. Not her father, not Jim. And not even Jessica and Elizabeth, who she'd thought were her friends. She felt very alone just then.

But the next time she turned around, she saw that Elizabeth, Jessica, and Amy had just moved down to stay dry. The three girls waved and smiled at her and she waved back.

It was raining harder now, and the base paths were getting muddy. Coach Andrews stood up and strode to the plate for a conference with the opposing coach and the umpire. A moment later, the umpire held up his arms to signal that the game had been called off.

Coach Andrews came back to the bench. "OK, everybody," he said, pulling his cap down over his eyes. "That's it for today. We're rescheduling for tomorrow, weather permitting. I'll see you at one for warm-up." He turned and looked directly at Billie. "I'll decide on a starting pitcher tomorrow."

Billie sucked in her breath. At least there was one consolation out of all this rainy, muddy mess. If the coach started her tomorrow (a *big* if), maybe she could redeem herself. She turned to say goodbye to Jim. He was searching the stands for Sally, and Billie couldn't resist grinning. She wasn't the only one who'd been deserted by a bunch of fair-weather fans.

Jessica and Amy had come down to the field to get Billie and the duffle bag that had her party dress and her shoes in it. Elizabeth had gone to the concession stand to call Mr. Wakefield for a ride.

"I don't feel much like a party right now," Billie said with a sigh, as the car headed toward the Wakefields'. Her hair hung in limp, wet strands around her shoulders. "I sure don't look ready for a party," she added glumly. "Besides, my dress is probably ruined from being stuffed in that duffle bag. Maybe I'd just better call my mom when we get to your house and have her come and get me."

"Don't be silly," Jessica said with breezy confidence, as Mr. Wakefield parked the maroon van in the driveway. "We know how to fix messy hair and wrinkled dresses, don't we,

Elizabeth?" They got out and went upstairs to Elizabeth's room.

"I'll take care of your dress," Elizabeth said, reaching for Billie's duffle bag. She opened it and pulled out the dress, the shoes, and the present that Billie's mom had wrapped for Julie. "Why don't you take a hot shower?" she suggested to Billie.

Billie sighed and sat down to peel off her wet socks. The twins were determined to take her to Julie's party. After all, they'd helped her buy her dress. And Jessica had organized the girls to cheer at the game.

A few minutes later, wrapped in a fluffy pink towel, Billie was sitting in front of the mirror in Elizabeth's room, while Jessica rolled her hair up on curlers.

"What are you doing to my hair?" Billie asked. The curlers made her scalp feel tight and itchy.

"Oh, just wait and see," Jessica replied airily. "It's a surprise."

Just as Jessica was finishing Billie's hair, Elizabeth came back in and hung the freshly pressed dress on the closet door. "There, you see?" she said proudly, straightening the velvet ribbons. "Good as new."

Billie had to admit it, the dress looked even prettier than it had in the store. One thing was for sure: she never would have bought *this* dress if it hadn't been for Jessica and Elizabeth.

While Jessica was taking out Billie's curlers and combing Billie's hair, Elizabeth was putting on a red dress with a matching scarf.

"Can I look in the mirror now?" Billie asked nervously.

Jessica pretended to give the matter serious thought. "Do you think we should let her look?" she asked Elizabeth.

"I don't think she's ready yet," Elizabeth said. "She needs to put her dress and shoes on."

Billie put on her dress and white panty-hose. Then she slipped her shoes on and turned to the twins. With great anticipation she asked, "Now can I look?"

But Jessica shook her head no, and picked up a tube of lip gloss.

"Wait a minute," Billie objected, raising her hand. "You guys are going too far. I mean, curling my hair is one thing, but I've *never* worn makeup."

Jessica brushed Billie's objection aside. "There's a first time for everything. And anyway, it's just a little lip gloss. After all, you *are* twelve, you know."

"I think it's OK, Billie," Elizabeth added reassuringly. "Jessica won't put on too much."

Billie sighed and sat down on the bed to submit to Jessica's makeup artistry.

"There," Jessica announced, when she was finished. She pulled Billie up to her feet. "We're ready for the great moment!"

"Wait," Elizabeth said, hurrying to her dresser. "I've got something I want Billie to wear." She took a pearl bracelet out of her jewelry box and slipped it on Billie's arm. "This is for luck," she said.

"Hey, that makes me think of something too," Jessica said. She disappeared and came back carrying a pair of tiny pearl earrings that she clipped onto Billie's earlobes.

Billie looked down at the bracelet on her arm. "Hey, you guys," she said softly, "this is really nice of you." She looked at the two of them. They were the greatest friends she'd ever had.

"*Now* do you think we're ready?" Jessica asked Elizabeth.

Elizabeth turned the mirror to face Billie. "Presenting the new Billie!" she said, with a smile.

Billie gasped. The last time she'd seen her reflection, a bedraggled baseball pitcher with limp, straggly hair had stared back at her. But now, in her place, stood a dressed-up girl with light brown curls tumbling around her face, her cheeks glowing, and her eyes shining like stars.

"Billie," Jessica and Elizabeth said in unison, "you look beautiful!"

Billie, appraising herself in the mirror, could only agree. She touched the tiny earrings and then turned to Elizabeth's bracelet on her arm, admiring its soft pearly glow.

She felt strange and wonderful at the same time, and almost as good as if she had pitched a no-hitter.

# Nine

◇

"See? I *told* you she'd look great!" Jessica whispered to Elizabeth as they followed Billie down the stairs. "Just wait until Jim Sturbridge sees her! He'll drop Sally so fast that—"

Elizabeth stopped in the middle of the stairs. "Jessica, you promised," she said accusingly. "You swore you wouldn't interfere."

"I'm not going to interfere," she said. "I'm just making a prediction, that's all. Billie Layton is much cuter than Sally Holcomb, and Jim is sure to notice at the party."

At the foot of the stairs, Mr. Wakefield was waiting. "Ready, girls?" he said. Billie saw his expression change as she reached the bottom step. His eyes widened, and then he whistled, slowly, under his breath.

"Is *this* the same Billie Layton who drove

home with us a little while ago?" he asked. "The Little League pitcher?"

Billie felt herself blushing. She stole a shy glance at Jessica and Elizabeth. They were smiling proudly. "The very same one," Elizabeth said, putting her arm around Billie.

Mr. Wakefield opened the door for them, grinning from ear to ear. "I just hope that Sweet Valley is ready for you three beautiful girls." With that, they went out to the van and climbed in.

As they rode to Julie's house, Billie realized she hadn't really thought about the party yet. She had no idea what to expect.

When the girls arrived, they gave Julie their presents and were led to a large game room at the back of the house. One of the boys was playing DJ with Julie's stereo and some kids were dancing. A group was gathered around a Ping-Pong table, and toward the back of the room there was a table piled high with sandwiches, chips, cookies, and soda.

Billie hung back shyly. "Come on," Elizabeth coaxed. "You know everybody here. Let's go watch the Ping-Pong tournament."

After a few minutes, somebody thrust a

Ping-Pong paddle into Billie's hand, and before she realized what had happened, she had won three straight games. Her fastball might have evaporated on her, but she was still a pretty mean Ping-Pong player!

In a short while, Billie had forgotten all about her new dress and her curls and her lipstick, and she'd almost stopped looking around to see whether Jim was there. So when Aaron Dallas came up and asked her to dance, she accepted immediately. After that, it was Tom McKay, and then Pete Stone. None of the boys, who were all fellow Rangers, said a word about the game. They seemed to be happy just dancing with her, and Billie was having more fun than she could possibly have imagined.

In the corner by the food table, the Unicorns were all standing together. "Is that *really* Billie Layton over there?" Ellen Riteman asked Jessica, pointing to where Billie was dancing with Pete Stone.

Jessica nodded happily, munching on a chocolate-chip cookie. "It certainly is," she said. "Doesn't she look great?" She looked over at Sally Holcomb, who was wearing a peasant-style dress. Jim was with her, and they were talking.

"Billie looks *terrific!*" Mary Wallace exclaimed.

Even Lila had to concede that Billie looked nice. "It's certainly a change from the way she looked this afternoon," she admitted.

"And look at all the guys she's dancing with," Ellen remarked enviously. "Half the boys in this room are waiting in line. Even Colin Harmon wants a turn."

Mary smiled a little. "You know, maybe the Unicorns are missing out on something."

Lila looked at her suspiciously. "Missing out?" she asked. She sounded a little worried. "What could we possibly be missing out on?"

"Well," Mary began, "we have lots of talented people in the club, but Jessica is our only athlete and athletes *are* pretty special. Maybe we ought to invite Billie to become a Unicorn."

Ellen Riteman looked thoughtful. "I see what you mean," she said. "And it was sort of fun cheering at the ball game—at least, until it started to rain. Maybe it would have been even more fun if we'd been cheering for a fellow Unicorn."

But Lila wasn't so sure. "Let's not be too hasty," she cautioned. "I think we should wait and see how Billie does at the game tomorrow. I, for one, really don't care all that much about baseball." She smiled at Jessica. "I just went to the game as a favor to Jessica."

Jessica sighed. It was clear that the Unicorns really weren't interested in doing nice things for other people—not yet, anyway. She glanced over toward the spot where she had seen Jim and Sally a minute before. They were still there. It didn't look as if Jim even knew that Billie was in the room.

She had to figure out some way to get Jim and Billie together.

Out on the dance floor, Billie breathlessly turned down Tommy Parks' request for another dance and made her way to a seat in the corner to rest. Tommy followed her, insisting on getting her a soft drink.

She looked around the room at all of the familiar people. She still couldn't get over how differently the boys were treating her! She played ball with some of them at least twice a week, and although they were always friendly on the field, they had never been so attentive! The thought of Tommy Parks rushing off to get her an orange drink made her want to giggle with delight. She could feel her cheeks getting pink.

Just then, Billie heard Sally Holcomb's unmistakable laugh. She looked up and saw her over in the corner talking to Jim. Sally's bright red-and-yellow peasant dress revealed her shoulders and made her look at least fourteen. All of a sudden Billie's own dress, which had seemed so grown-up and beautiful a moment ago, seemed babyish in comparison.

Jim looked up just then, and stared straight at her. Forcing herself to smile, Billie waved. But Jim didn't wave back. He just stared at her with a kind of curious look, as if he were looking at a stranger. Then, he turned his back to say something to Jessica, who had just come up beside him.

The excitement Billie had been feeling turned to instant gloom. It was nice that all the boys paid attention to her. But she had to admit it was Jim's attention she wanted. And it was very clear he was too busy to even say hello to her.

Without waiting to tell Tommy she didn't want the orange drink, Billie crossed the room and went into the hallway, blinking back the tears. She was trying so hard not to cry she didn't pay any attention when Jim looked at her with a shock of recognition on his face. She didn't even see him take two steps toward her, with his hand out.

Billie just kept on walking down the hallway, heading for the front door.

"You're not leaving so soon, are you, Billie?" It was Mrs. Porter, standing beside the stairs. She sounded concerned.

Billie took a deep breath. "I . . . I have to," she said. "I have to go home. Thank you for the lovely party."

At that moment, the doorbell rang. Mrs. Porter opened the door.

"I'm Commander Layton. Is my daughter here?"

Mrs. Porter stepped back. "Yes, she's right here," she said.

Billie blinked in surprise. "Daddy!" she exclaimed. "What are *you* doing here?"

There was a worried crease between her father's eyes. "I've come to get you," he said.

"To get me?" Billie's heart was beginning to pound. "Is there something wrong?"

"No," he said. "At least, I hope not. I've just taken your mother to the hospital. Your little brother is on his way!"

# Ten

◇

Billie's mother had decided to have her baby in a special area of the hospital called "The Stork Club." It was on a floor adjacent to the regular maternity rooms and the delivery room, but "The Stork Club" was completely different. Instead of the stark white walls and ceilings that she had imagined, her mother's two-room suite was more like a hotel room. There was a sofa, a TV set, and photos of babies on the wall. There was even a little refrigerator and a hot plate in the corner.

"The Stork Club" was different in another way, too, as Commander Layton explained to Billie. In this part of the hospital, she would get to hold her baby brother as soon as he was born.

"Me? *Hold* the baby?" Billie asked in alarm. "If it's all the same to you, Dad, I don't think I want to hold him right away."

Her father didn't respond. "Margaret?" he called, opening a door to another room. "Billie's here." He opened the door wider and ushered Billie in. "I'm going down to the snack bar for a few minutes," he announced. Then he left and Billie found herself alone with her mother. She had expected her to look sick or worried, but she didn't at all. Her cheeks were pink and she seemed excited and expectant, lying in a bed that was made with pretty, pink-flowered sheets. She was wearing her favorite pink night-gown, and there was a bouquet of flowers on the bedside table. Beside the bed stood a little wicker bassinet, already made up with blue sheets and a blue blanket.

Happily, Billie's mother held out her arms. "There you are," she said, "my favorite daughter!" And then her eyes lit up with surprise and admiration as she gazed at Billie.

"Oh, Belinda!" she exclaimed. "You look so pretty! Your dress is simply beautiful—and your *hair*!"

Billie couldn't help smiling at her mother's surprise. "Jessica curled it," she said, patting the light brown ringlets on her shoulders. "And Elizabeth helped, too."

"What fun!" her mother exclaimed. "And how was the game? Did you win? I'm awfully sorry that Dad didn't make it, honey. He wanted to wait and hear what the doctor had to say."

"Oh, that's OK," Billie said, waving her hand. "We got rained out, anyway." She gave her mother a close look. "We got rescheduled for tomorrow. Do you think he can come then?" She wasn't quite sure why she asked. Things had been so bad today that maybe Coach Andrews wouldn't even want to start her tomorrow.

"I'm sure he can come," her mother said. She sighed and patted her tummy under the sheet. Billie saw that there were little tears— tears of happiness—in the corners of her eyes. "I can't *imagine* a nicer time than being here with my grown-up daughter, waiting for her little brother to arrive!"

Suddenly, neither could Billie. It seemed like the most exciting moment in the whole world. And somehow, it also seemed like the perfect moment to tell her mother about getting her period.

When she finished the whole story, her

mother squeezed her hand. "My *very* grown-up daughter," she murmured with a big smile.

At that moment, Billie's father came back, with hot coffee for himself and an orange drink and a magazine for Billie. Commander Layton started talking about the things all four of them would do together, but Billie's mind kept wandering.

"And when he gets a little older," Billie's father continued, "you can show him your famous fastball."

Billie made a face. "My not-so-famous fastball," she mumbled, thinking about that afternoon.

But suddenly it didn't seem very important. She had pitched a couple of bad innings. So what? After all, even the best pitchers in the world had a bad day once in a while. And as for Jim Sturbridge and Sally Holcomb—well, that was something she could probably get used to, as long as she and Jim could still talk about baseball once in a while.

A little while later, the doctor arrived with two nurses, all dressed in green pants and green smocks. Billie kissed her mom and took her orange drink into the other room. She sat

down on the sofa with her favorite magazine—
*Sports Illustrated*—open on her lap. There was a
great story about one of her all-time favorite
baseball heroes.

Billie had a hard time keeping her mind on
the article, though. She was exhausted from the
events of the day. Sleepily, she curled up in a
corner of the sofa. Maybe she could take a quick
nap. She dreamed she heard a baby crying,
sweet and far away, and she curled up tighter,
feeling warm and happy. It was a nice sound.

Then she felt her father gently shaking her
shoulder, and realized she hadn't dreamed it
after all!

"Wake up, honey," he said, "your brother's
here!" He was beaming from ear to ear. "Big
and healthy and ready for anything!"

Billie sat up straight and rubbed her eyes.

Her father held out his hand. "Come and
see," he invited.

Tiptoeing gingerly, Billie went into the other
room. Her mother was sitting up in the bed,
looking a little tired but very happy. In the crook
of her arm, she was holding a tiny baby,
wrapped in a soft blue blanket.

Billie sat down on the edge of the bed, a

new and very strange feeling flooding through her. She stared at the baby, her new little brother, as he waved one tiny fist and made a sucking noise with his lips. He was the most helpless little creature she had ever seen, and her heart was filled with love for him.

"Would you like to hold him?" her mother asked softly.

Billie looked up at her father with a worried frown. "Do you think it's OK?" she asked. "I mean, I won't hurt him or anything, will I?"

"I'm *sure* you won't hurt him," her father said. "Babies are tougher than you think." He smiled. "You certainly were. You were one tough little kid." He looked at her. "Cute, too."

Billie couldn't help laughing. But she stopped laughing when her father picked up the baby from her mother and put him in Billie's arms.

"Here you are," he said. "Meet your brother, William Arthur Layton."

Billie leaned over the baby, cuddling him close and making comforting noises. All the jealous thoughts she'd had about him were forgotten. He was her very own baby brother. It seemed like a miracle.

# Eleven

As Billie sat on the bed, her father stepped back, looking at the two of them together. He smiled for a moment, and then his expression suddenly changed to surprise. He whistled softly. "Hey," he said, "who's this beautiful, dressed-up young lady?"

Billie looked up, startled. "What?" she asked. She looked around the room.

"He means *you*, honey," Mrs. Layton said, laughing. "I guess he hasn't seen you in a dress lately."

Commander Layton shook his head in surprise. "I know I've had a lot on my mind this afternoon," he said, "but how could I have missed . . . ?" He grinned and touched Billie's curls. "Margaret, she has your hair, and your complexion, too." He whistled again, in admiration. "She's going to be a beauty when she grows up, just like you."

"She *is* grown up," her mother said, very softly, with a special look at Billie. "She's a young lady now."

"You're right," her father said. "She is, indeed. And a very beautiful young lady, at that!"

As Billie held the baby, her father bent over and hugged and kissed her. She realized that this was the very first time she'd ever gotten his attention as a *girl*. He'd always complimented her on her athletic abilities, but none of those compliments had ever been as sweet as the one he paid her just now.

"I think," her mother said, "that if you two don't mind, the baby and I would like to have a little nap now." She smiled at Billie. "Would you put him in his basket for me, honey?"

Carefully, as if she were holding an armful of robin's eggs, Billie put the baby into the basket and loosened his blanket. Just at that moment, a blissful smile crossed his face and he opened his eyes.

"He smiled at me!" Billie exclaimed excitedly. "And he's got blue eyes!"

Her mother laughed as she snuggled into

the pillows. "I expect that that smile is here to stay."

Billie's father held out his hand. "Come on, Billie. Let's let these guys get some rest, huh?"

Billie pulled herself up straighter as they left the room. "Actually," she said, "I think I'm getting a little too old for a nickname like that. Can you call me Belinda? Besides, we've got a real little Billy in the family now. It would be pretty confusing if there were two of us."

Commander Layton laughed huskily and put his hand on her shoulder. "You sure about that, Bil—Belinda?" he asked.

"I'm sure," Belinda said. And she was.

As they got into the car to go home, her father suddenly looked stricken.

"You know," he said, "in all the excitement this afternoon, I forgot all about the baseball game! I'm really sorry I missed it, Belinda."

"You don't have to be sorry," she told him. "You didn't miss a thing. We got rained out so we'll be playing tomorrow. That means we can't go fishing, but I guess we'd have postponed the trip anyway since Billy arrived early. Mom said you could probably make the game, though."

Commander Layton nodded as he started

the car. "I'm sure I can. Are you pitching again?"

Belinda shrugged. "I don't know," she said. "I had a couple of bad innings this afternoon. Maybe Coach Andrews will decide to start Dennis instead."

"Well, I'll be there," her father promised. "I'll be cheering for you." He stole a sideways glance at her. "Hey," he said, "I'm really hungry. In fact, I'm starving. What do you say we stop for a pizza? With a double order of anchovies?"

Belinda giggled. She and her father both loved anchovies. "That would be great," she said happily. "A double order of anchovies."

On Sunday, there was a not a single cloud in the sky and the sun shone brightly in Sweet Valley. Belinda was at the field at one o'clock sharp. Her newly-washed uniform was clean and white and she'd pulled her still-curled hair back into her usual ponytail. She hadn't been able to resist using just a little dab of lip gloss that she'd found on her mother's dressing table, and one tiny squirt of perfume.

As she got out of the car and began to trot

toward the home side of the park, she ran into Pete Stone, who played center field.

"Hi," Pete said. He was staring at her.

"Hi," Belinda said, suddenly feeling shy.

Pete cleared his throat. "Listen," he said, "I was wondering . . . Uh, maybe you'd like to go over to Casey's after the game for some ice cream?"

"Hey, thanks," Belinda replied. "Can I take a rain check? My dad and I are going to the hospital to see my new little brother."

Pete grinned. "A new brother, huh?" He gave her an admiring look. "Well, he's got a heck of a lot to live up to."

Belinda shot the grin back. "Thanks," she said. Pete's compliment made her feel good all over.

Coach Andrews was standing by the bench when she came up, her glove in one hand and a ball in the other. "Well," he asked, squinting at her, "how does that arm feel today, Billie?"

Belinda looked up at him. "Would you mind," she said sweetly, "calling me Belinda? That's my real name, after all. And I've got a new brother—we're calling *him* Billy."

The coach blinked. "Yeah, sure," he said. "Well, what do you think, Belinda? How's the arm? Feel like you can start for us today?"

Belinda grinned confidently. "Sure, I can start," she said, smacking the ball into her glove, hard. "The arm feels great! Better than ever, in fact."

The coach slapped her on the back. "OK, then, you're on. You and Jim warm up, huh?"

As Belinda spun around to start warming up, she spotted Jessica and Elizabeth in the stands. Her father was sitting on the same bench, eating a hot dog. He waved at her with a proud grin on his face and held up two fingers in a V, for victory.

Jim was buckling on his face mask when Belinda found him. "Coach says for us to warm up," she said briefly. "I'm starting this afternoon."

Jim's face broke into a broad grin. "Hey, that's great!" he said. Then his grin turned sheepish and his ears began to grow pink. "Uh, about yesterday—" he began.

Belinda took a deep breath. *Why did he have to bring that up?* "I know I didn't do so well yesterday," she admitted. "But today's going to be a lot better." She rubbed her arm, feeling the strength and power in it. "I can *feel* it."

"No, no," Jim said, flushing deep red. "I don't mean about what happened at the game. I'm talking about the party."

Then Belinda remembered. Jim and Sally. The look on Jim's face when he looked at her, as if he were looking at a stranger.

"Oh, that," she said flatly. He didn't need to bring *that* up, either. It was over with, and best forgotten.

But Jim was insistent. "I just wanted to say that I didn't recognize you yesterday afternoon at the party, that's all. I mean, you were so pretty in that blue dress, with your hair all curled. You looked so *different*. I didn't even know it was you until Jessica told me. I went looking for you then, but I couldn't find you anywhere. Then somebody said you'd left." He looked down at the dirt and drew a circle in it with the toe of his sneaker. "I was sorry you'd gone," he said. "I wanted to ask you to dance."

"You did?" Belinda asked delightedly. "You really did? Honest?"

Jim looked at her, his eyes very serious.

"Yeah," he replied. "I really did. Honest." He flashed her a grin.

"Thanks for telling me, Sturbridge," Belinda said. She took a dozen running steps backward and tossed the ball at Jim. He caught it and plopped it a couple of times in his mitt, getting the feel of it. Behind his mask, he was grinning.

"OK, Layton," he challenged, lobbing the ball back to her. "Let's see what you've got on the ball today!"

What Belinda had on the ball today was *lots* of steam. Her fastball sizzled and her curve dropped as if it had a magnetic attraction to home plate. Hardly anyone got to first base. And when the game was all over, the score was Rangers eight, Rebels nothing. It was a solid shutout!

Behind the plate, Jim yanked off his mask and rushed out to hug Belinda. "Great game!" he shouted. Tom McKay dashed in from second base, and Pete Stone from center field, and they all did an impromptu dance on the pitcher's mound. Up in the bleachers, Jessica was leading the Ranger fans in a victory cheer.

But Belinda was happiest when she saw her father. He had borrowed a pom-pom and was waving it wildly, and she could hear his voice over all the others.

"Hooray, *Belinda!*" he shouted. "Way to go, Belinda!"

# Twelve

◇

The next day, Jessica and Belinda carried their lunch trays to a table where several of the Unicorns were talking about Ellen Riteman's new idea.

"A birthday-party service?" Jessica asked, opening her milk carton.

Ellen nodded. "Sure. Mothers who want to give a birthday party for their kids could call us, and we'd do the whole thing. Balloons, games, refreshments, decorations. They'd pay us, and we'd donate the money to Sweet Valley Middle School. That way we'd be *sure* to win the Service Award!"

Jessica put her milk down and clapped delightedly. "Ellen," she crowed, "that's a fabulous idea! Parties are *exactly* what the Unicorns do best. We'd make tons of money—and it would be great for our image!"

"Just think what a glorious new image we'd have!" Lila chimed in.

Janet looked up from her plate of spaghetti. "Let's put Ellen's suggestion at the top of the agenda for our next meeting," she said. She turned to Belinda. "Right now, we've got something else we need to take care of."

Belinda looked around the table, feeling a little uncomfortable. She wasn't sure why Jessica had invited her to eat with the Unicorns.

Janet cleared her throat and sat up straight. "Belinda Layton," she said, in an authoritative voice, "you've been asked here for a very important reason. In view of your extra-special accomplishments, the Unicorns have chosen *you* to become a member of the club."

Belinda stared at Janet. "A . . . a member?" she squeaked. "Of the *Unicorns*?"

Jessica nudged her. "Say yes," she whispered. "That way we can spend more time together."

Janet began talking about what a privilege and honor it was to become a member of the Unicorns, and how the Unicorns were all unique and special. She went on and on, but Belinda scarcely heard her. Then Janet paused and looked at Belinda. It was obvious that she was waiting for an answer.

Belinda looked around the table. The other girls were watching her expectantly, and she felt a flush of pride. Belinda Layton, a Unicorn!

"Yes," she said happily. "Yes, I'd *love* to be a Unicorn."

Jessica threw her arms around her. "Oh, Belinda," she said ecstatically, "this is *wonderful!*"

After lunch, Jessica and Belinda put their dishes on the conveyer belt. "Are you going to the concert next week?" Belinda asked. "My mom said she already has a list of books she plans to order for the school library." Sweet Valley Middle School had organized a rock concert featuring a very popular high school band, The Wild Ones, in order to raise money for new library books.

Jessica nodded. "The concert's going to be a lot of fun," she said. "I can't wait to see that gorgeous lead singer up close. I've already planned what I'm going to wear."

Behind them, Ellen Riteman spoke up. "And Secca Lake is a perfect setting for a concert. *Everybody* will be there."

"Everybody but me," a gloomy voice said behind them. With a noisy crash, a boy dumped a load of dishes on the conveyor belt.

Jessica spun around. "Patrick Morris," she exclaimed, "why won't *you* be there? It's one of the biggest events of the year. Everyone's looking forward to it."

Patrick looked down at his feet. "I guess I shouldn't have said anything," he mumbled.

Jessica studied him. "But you have to come," she insisted.

Patrick threw her a miserable glance. "My folks won't let me go," he said. "They say the concert will go on past my curfew."

"Curfew?" Jessica could hardly believe her ears. "Curfews went out with the Dark Ages!"

"Not at *my* house they didn't," Patrick said. "Curfews, rules, regulations—you name it, my parents have a rule for it, with *no* exceptions." He turned and walked away with his hands deep in his pockets, his head bowed.

"Ugh," Belinda breathed, "how awful! Can you imagine having such *strict* parents?"

Jessica thought of her wonderful parents, always so understanding, always ready to listen when she had a problem. She stared after Patrick's retreating figure.

"No," she said, "I can't imagine it." *Poor Patrick,* she thought. *Living in his house must be like living in a prison. There ought to be a law against parents like that!*

**How will Patrick react to his parents' strict rules? Find out in Sweet Valley Twins #26, TAKING CHARGE.**

# YOUR OWN

## SLAM BOOK!

If you've read *Slambook Fever*, Sweet Valley High #48, you know that slam books are the rage at Sweet Valley High. Now *you* can have a slam book of your own! Make up your own categories, such as "Biggest Jock" or "Best Looking," and have your friends fill in the rest! There's a four-page calendar, horoscopes and questions most asked by Sweet Valley readers with answers from Elizabeth and Jessica

### It's a must for SWEET VALLEY fans!

☐ 05496- **FRANCINE PASCAL'S SWEET VALLEY HIGH SLAM BOOK**
**Laurie Pascal Wenk**                                    **$3.95**

---

Bantam Books, Dept. SVS6, 414 East Golf Road, Des Plaines, IL 60016

Please send me the books I have checked above. I am enclosing $_____ (please add $2.00 to cover postage and handling). Send check or money order— no cash or C.O.D.s please.

Mr/Ms _____

Address _____

City/State _____ Zip _____

SVS6—1/89

Please allow four to six weeks for delivery. This offer expires 7/89.

# THE CLASS TRIP

## SWEET VALLEY TWINS SUPER EDITION #1

Join Jessica and Elizabeth in the very first SWEET
VALLEY TWINS Super Edition—it's longer, can be read
out of sequence, and is full of page-turning excitement!

The day of the big sixth-grade class trip to the
Enchanted Forest is finally here! But Jessica and
Elizabeth have a fight and spend the beginning of
the trip arguing. When Elizabeth decides to make
up, Jessica has disappeared. In a frantic search for
her sister, Elizabeth finds herself in a series of
dangerous and exciting Alice In Wonderland-type of
adventures.

☐ 15588-1  $2.95/$3.50 in Canada

Buy them at your local bookstore or use this
page to order.

------------------------------------------------

Bantam Books, Dept. SVT4, 414 East Golf Road, Des Plaines, IL 60016

Please send me the book I have checked above. I am enclosing $_____
(please add $2.00 to cover postage and handling). Send check or money
order—no cash or C.O.D.s please.

Mr/Ms _____

Address _____

City/State _____ Zip _____

SVT4—11/88

Please allow four to six weeks for delivery. This offer expires 5/89.

# IT ALL STARTED WITH THE

**F**rancine Pascal introduces you to Jessica and Elizabeth when they were 12, facing the same problems with their folks and friends that you do.

---

Bantam Books, Dept. SVT, 414 East Golf Road, Des Plaines, IL 60016

Please send me the books I have checked above. I am enclosing $_____ (please add $2.00 to cover postage and handling). Send check or money order—no cash or C.O.D.s please.

Mr/Ms _____

Address _____

City/State _____ Zip _____

SVT—10/88

Please allow four to six weeks for delivery. This offer expires 4/89.

# Special Offer
# Buy a Bantam Book
# *for only 50¢.*

Now you can order the exciting books you've
been wanting to read straight from Bantam's
latest catalog of hundreds of titles. *And* this
special offer gives you the opportunity to purchase
a Bantam book for only 50¢. Here's how:

By ordering any five books at the regular
price per order, you can also choose any other
single book listed (up to a $5.95 value) for only
50¢. Some restrictions do apply, so for further
details send for Bantam's catalog of titles today.

Just send us your name and address and
we'll send you Bantam Book's SHOP AT
HOME CATALOG!

BANTAM BOOKS, INC.
P.O. Box 1006, South Holland, Ill. 60473

Mr./Mrs./Ms. _____
(please print)

Address _____

City _____ State _____ Zip _____
FC(B)—10/87

Printed in the U.S.A.     *BANTAM* 🐓 *BOOKS*